why?

A Story for Kids Who Have
Lost a Parent to Suicide

by Melissa Allen Heath, PhD
illustrated by Frances Ives

Magination Press ◆ Washington, DC
American Psychological Association

Dedicated to my children, Joni and Austin—MAH

For anyone affected by the darkness—FI

Books for Kids From the
American Psychological Association

Magination Press is a registered trademark of the American Psychological Association.
Order books at maginationpress.org, or call 1-800-374-2721.

Book design by Christina Gaugler
Printed by Lake Book Manufacturing, LLC, Melrose Park, IL

Library of Congress Cataloging-in-Publication Data

Names: Heath, Melissa Allen, author. | Ives, Frances, illustrator.
Title: Why? : a book for kids who have lost a parent to suicide / by Melissa Allen Heath, PhD ; illustrated by Frances Ives.
Description: Washington, DC : Magination Press, [2023] | «American Psychological Association.»
Summary: With help from his mother, a young boy named Oliver copes with the suicide of his father.
Identifiers: LCCN 2023006562 (print) | LCCN 2023006563 (ebook) | ISBN 9781433841965 (hardback) | ISBN 9781433841972 (ebook)
Subjects: CYAC: Grief—Fiction. | Suicide—Fiction. | Parent and child—Fiction. | LCGFT: Picture books.
Classification: LCC PZ7.1.H4325 Wh 2023 (print) | LCC PZ7.1.H4325 (ebook) | DDC [E]—dc23 LC record available at https://lccn.loc.gov/2023006562 LC ebook record available at https://lccn.loc.gov/2023006563

Manufactured in the United States of America

10 9 8 7 6 5 4 3 2 1

Oliver's mommy says when he was a baby,
his daddy loved holding him.

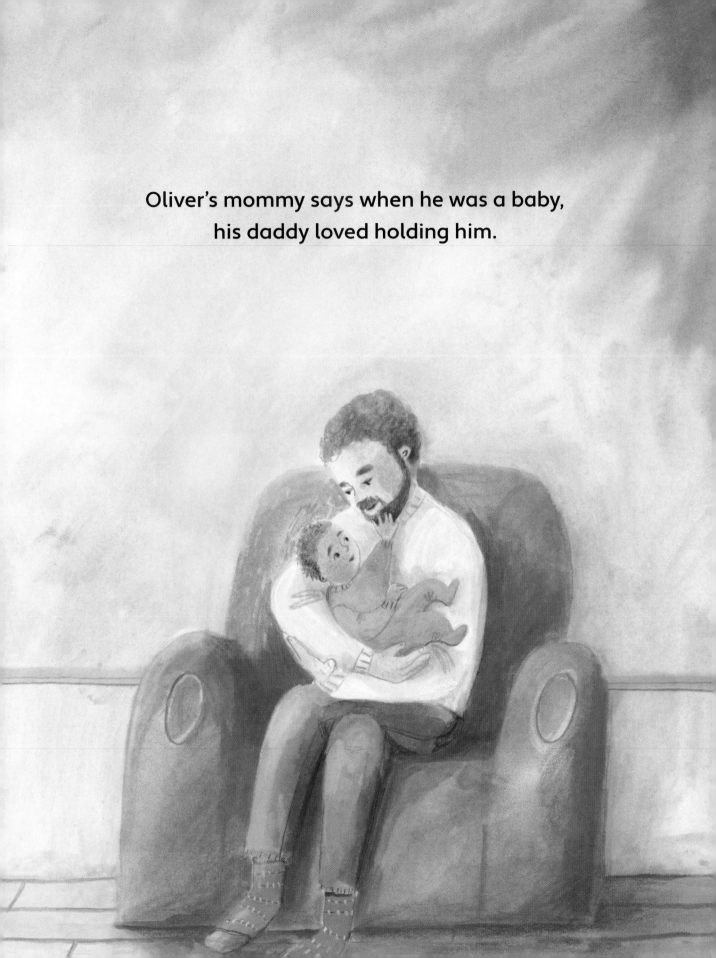

...Before his daddy
went to work.

...As soon as his daddy
got home from work.

...When his daddy watched a football game.

...When Oliver cried in the middle of the night.

Oliver's mommy says
his daddy loved him—
a whole bunch, forever
and for always.

Oliver's mommy says he has his daddy's eyes.

She says he has his daddy's hair.

Oliver even has his daddy's name.

But Oliver's daddy is not here.
He is gone. He died. He is dead.

Why?

When Oliver asks, "Why?" his mommy cries.

Oliver cries when his mommy cries.

They both cry. His mommy
cuddles him very close.

It is hard to ask "Why?"
But Oliver knows his mommy
will answer his question.

So, Oliver asks, "Why?"

His mommy hugs him tight,
then she tells him why.

"Daddy had a serious illness called depression. Oliver, do not worry, you cannot catch depression from another person."

"Daddy felt overwhelmed by a deep dark sadness. Many people get better with medicine and treatment, but that did not help your daddy."

"He said everything felt dark."

"He was stuck in that deep dark sadness and thought he would never get unstuck."

Oliver asks, "Why did he die?"

This part is hard for Oliver and his mommy. It is hard thinking about it. It is even harder talking about it. But this is what happened.

Oliver's daddy died by suicide. Daddy made his body stop working. His brain stopped. He stopped breathing. His body died.

Oliver's mommy says his daddy did not want to leave Oliver and his mommy. He died to get away from the sad, scary, and dark feelings. He died to stop the deep dark sadness.

Oliver and his mommy are so sad.
His daddy died. It is not Oliver's fault.
It is not Mommy's fault.

With the warmest of hugs, Oliver's mommy says, "He loved you. That will never change."

Even though Oliver's daddy is dead, they think of him. They remember him. Sometimes Oliver and his mommy go to visit a gravestone with his daddy's name.

Sometimes, mixed with sadness, they also try to remember happy times.

Oliver's mommy says Daddy liked to hold Oliver...

before Daddy went to work, as soon as Daddy got home from work,

when Daddy watched a football game, and when Oliver cried in the middle of the night.

Oliver's mommy says Daddy loved him.

She tells Oliver, "You have his eyes."

"You have his hair."

"Oliver, you even have his name."

Oliver has pictures of his daddy before
he got stuck in deep dark sadness.
He had a beautiful smile. He was happy.

Oliver cries with his mommy, but not all the time.

They have many pictures of their family smiling and laughing.

When they look at those pictures, they smile and laugh.

Oliver's daddy is still his daddy.

He always will be.

Oliver and his mommy will always love Daddy...
a whole bunch, forever and for always.

Reader's Note

Of all challenges children may face, the death of a parent is one of the most traumatic. In particular, a parent's death by suicide poses unique challenges for child survivors. In comparison to the general public, child survivors may experience an increased risk for anxiety and depression; lower self-esteem; and higher levels of self-blame, anger, and shame. Although negative ramifications of a parent's suicide are potentially significant, caring adults and the surviving parent have the power to intervene, open communication about the suicide, and provide much-needed ongoing emotional support. This support strengthens children's resilience and adaptive coping. Furthermore, this support strengthens family relationships and decreases feelings of isolation and stigmatization.

Following a parent's suicide, open communication lays the foundation for healing. However, because suicide is a highly stigmatized topic, many people may avoid talking about it. Additionally, family secrets surrounding the parent's suicide, though intended to protect the child from the harsh reality of suicide, may in the long run erode trust and block communication. Lacking opportunities to talk about their parent's suicide, many child survivors shoulder their grief in isolation. Though talking about suicide is difficult, encouraging open communication expands opportunities for children to adaptively process their grief. As children grieve, they need reassurance that it is not their fault. It is also not the surviving parent's fault.

Child survivors have a heightened awareness of the surviving parent's needs; for example, children may find it difficult to talk about a parent's suicide because they believe such conversation will make their surviving parent cry. Understandably, surviving parents are under immense pressure to manage their own grief while simultaneously bearing the many responsibilities of childcare and work. However, all suicide survivors—regardless of age—need to know that crying and strong emotions are typical reactions and should be accepted and expressed rather than denied and avoided. Surviving parents must allow themselves and their children opportunities to express strong emotions as they gather strength from one another, trusted family and friends, and professionals. Surviving parents model emotional expression as they explain to their children, "I cry because I am sad. This is a tough time for our family, but I am OK and we will be OK." "It is OK to grieve and share our feelings." By reaching out and seeking support, survivors show strength and over time emotional burdens become lighter.

Support Children in Addressing the Tasks of Grief

Parents and primary caregivers play a critical role in children's lives. During tough times children look to their caregivers for stability, guidance, and nurturance. The following sections are aligned with Worden's (1996) four *tasks of grief*: (a) accepting the reality of the parent's suicide; (b) facing grief and emotional pain (with support), rather than avoiding the pain; (c) adjusting to changes following the parent's suicide; and (d) remembering and memorializing the deceased parent. These tasks of grief are best navigated with the support of trusted adults that include the surviving parent and primary caregivers who love and care for the child. The following interventions target specific needs of child survivors.

Help Children Accept the Reality of Death

Regardless of age, children have difficulty facing the reality of a loved one's death. The reality of a parent dying by suicide is especially hard for children to understand and accept. Very young children have trouble understanding the permanence of death. Each morning they may wonder if the parent is alive. Each evening, they may wonder if their deceased parent will come home from work. The surviving parent and caregivers must be consistently patient and explain that when a person dies, their body quits working. With time and with repeated explanation, the maturing child will understand that their parent died, and that death is a part of life.

As a source of support, the surviving parent may consider their family's religious or spiritual beliefs and associated traditions. Others outside the family should be respectful of the family's beliefs and not offer conflicting information. The parent's religious or spiritual beliefs may offer hopeful views about a loving Supreme Being, life after death, and eventual reunification with loved ones. These beliefs and practices may support children in accepting the reality of death, answering questions about their deceased parent, and providing hope for the future.

One activity to help young children accept the reality of death is to grow annual flowers or plants. Explain that annual plants do not last through the cold winter, but seeds from those plants can be planted next spring or summer. This shows the cycle of life and death. Another option is to plant daffodils to show the cycle of life. As the family plants the seemingly lifeless bulbs, explain that this represents one stage of the plant's life. The flower will emerge each spring, bloom, then dry up and become dormant. Around the world, daffodils are a symbol of hope, renewal, and rebirth.

Help Children Face the Pain

Child survivors need support in facing emotional pain associated with death and suicide and being separated from their deceased parent. Talking about and expressing feelings helps children face their pain and process trauma and grief. Always acknowledge that facing emotional pain takes bravery and strength. As children face their emotional pain, they move forward. Caring adults need to send clear messages: "It's OK to talk about suicide." "It is OK to be angry." "It is OK to express feelings." "It is OK to cry." Also acknowledge that they are not alone as they experience their grief. Emphasize, "I am here for you." Also, teach and encourage simple relaxation skills. With young children, model and practice relaxation by slowly inhaling a deep breath, then while counting to 5, slowly exhale.

Additionally, connecting with others who have been through a similar experience helps normalize the trauma, helps survivors know that they are not alone in their pain, and reduces stigma. This is true for children and for parents. Some survivors may desire professional counseling provided in school-based settings or in the community. Others may participate in local suicide survivor support groups. *Interested parents can refer to the American Foundation for Suicide Prevention's website to locate the nearest suicide support group: afsp.org/find-a-support-group/*

Help Children Adjust to Change

Support children in adjusting to changes that occur following the parent's suicide. For example, financial security may be threatened, many families move, children change schools, surviving parents change jobs, and family dynamics change as the deceased parent's side of the family may blame the surviving spouse or may find it uncomfortable to interact with the children. Some changes may occur suddenly and out of necessity, other changes may occur across time. Although some changes are inevitable, keeping family routines and sticking to scheduled daily activities assures children that some things will not change. Most important of all, the surviving parent must always emphasize that their love is constant and consistent.

Help Children Remember and Memorialize

Immediately after the suicide, remembering and memorializing might be an especially hard task for survivors. However, eventually—as the reality of the situation sets in—parents and caregivers will be able to provide opportunities and encourage children to remember and memorialize the deceased parent. Although adults may understand that we carry the deceased person in our memory, this is difficult for a young child to understand. To encourage conversations about memories, look at pictures or photo albums, go through keepsakes, talk about the parent, and visit the cemetery. To help them remember, young children appreciate having a tangible object, such as locket with a small picture of their parent, a special stuffed toy, or a framed picture of their family during a happy time.

When to Seek Professional Support

In some situations, professional assistance may be needed. During the first few months following the parent's suicide, children's intense sadness is expected. However, when worrisome behaviors do not moderate, but continue to worsen over several months, parents become concerned. Some children have irregular sleep patterns and recurring nightmares. Some children struggle with anxiety and depression. Some children exhibit extreme behaviors. Others have little or no interest in activities they previously enjoyed.

When extreme or out-of-the-ordinary behaviors continue over time, parents may benefit from professional assistance or consultation. However, parents must reach out for immediate professional help when a child is preoccupied by death and suicide and makes comments such as, "Everyone would be better off without me," or "I do not want to live anymore." Professionals will guide parents and children through these critical situations. *Additionally, to provide more support and easier access, the US Suicide and Crisis Lifeline created a three-digit emergency phone number, 988. This phone number is available at all hours and provides translation for 250 languages. The Suicide and Crisis Lifeline is for those who feel that they—or their loved ones—are in a crisis situation.*

Surviving parents are not alone in supporting their young children. Mental health professionals in the school, community, and community support groups are available to listen to parent concerns and to offer guidance.

For More Information

A list of additional resources for supporting young child survivors—including a book list for children and a list of parent resources—is available at **apa.org/pubs/magination/why.**

Reference

Worden, J. W. (1996). *Children and grief: When a parent dies.* Guilford Press.

Melissa Allen Heath, PhD, is a licensed psychologist and a certified school psychologist. Her areas of expertise include bibliotherapy, social-emotional learning, suicide, anxiety, and bullying. She lives in McKinney, Texas.

Frances Ives is a freelance illustrator and artist. She earned her master's in children's book illustration from Cambridge School of Art. She lives in Cambridge, UK. Visit francesives.com.

Magination Press is the children's book imprint of the American Psychological Association. It's the combined power of psychology and literature that makes a Magination Press book special. Visit maginationpress.org and @MaginationPress on Facebook, Twitter, Instagram, and Pinterest.